Bayard Taylor

Home Ballads

Bayard Taylor

Home Ballads

ISBN/EAN: 9783743306080

Manufactured in Europe, USA, Canada, Australia, Japa

Cover: Foto ©Andreas Hilbeck / pixelio.de

Manufactured and distributed by brebook publishing software
(www.brebook.com)

Bayard Taylor

Home Ballads

HOME BALLADS

BY

BAYARD TAYLOR

WITH ILLUSTRATIONS

BOSTON
HOUGHTON, MIFFLIN AND COMPANY
The Riverside Press, Cambridge
1882

The Riverside Press, Cambridge :
Electrotyped and Printed by H. O. Houghton & Co.

CONTENTS.

———+———

LIST OF ILLUSTRATIONS.

THE
QUAKER
WIDOW

THE QUAKER WIDOW.

I.

THEE finds me in the garden, Hannah, — come in! 'T is kind of thee
To wait until the Friends were gone, who came to comfort me.
The still and quiet company a peace may give, indeed,
But blessed is the single heart that comes to us at need.

II.

Come, sit thee down! Here is the bench where Benjamin would sit
On First Day afternoons in spring, and watch the swallows flit:
He loved to smell the sprouting box, and hear the pleasant bees
Go humming round the lilacs and through the apple-trees.

III.

I think he loved the spring: not that he cared for flowers: most men
Think such things foolishness, — but we were first acquainted then,
One spring: the next he spoke his mind; the third I was his wife,
And in the spring (it happened so) our children entered life.

IV.

He was but seventy-five: I did not think to lay him yet
In Kennett graveyard, where at Monthly Meeting first we met.
The Father's mercy shows in this: 't is better I should be
Picked out to bear the heavy cross — alone in age — than he.

V.

We 've lived together fifty years: it seems but one long day,
One quiet Sabbath of the heart, till he was called away;
And as we bring from Meeting time a sweet contentment home,
So, Hannah, I have store of peace for all the days to come.

VI.

I mind (for I can tell thee now) how hard it was to know
If I had heard the spirit right, that told me I should go;
For father had a deep concern upon his mind that day,
But mother spoke for Benjamin, — she knew what best to say.

VII.

Then she was still: they sat awhile: at last she spoke again,
" The Lord incline thee to the right!" and " Thou shalt have him, Jane!"
My father said. I cried. Indeed, 't was not the least of shocks,
For Benjamin was Hicksite, and father Orthodox.

VIII.

I thought of this ten years ago, when daughter Ruth we lost:
Her husband's of the world, and yet I could not see her crossed.
She wears, thee knows, the gayest gowns, she hears a hireling priest, —
Ah, dear! the cross was ours: her life's a happy one, at least.

IX.

Perhaps she'll wear a plainer dress when she's as old as I, —
Would thee believe it, Hannah? once *I* felt temptation nigh!
My wedding-gown was ashen silk, too simple for my taste:
I wanted lace around the neck, and a ribbon at the waist.

X.

How strange it seemed to sit with him upon the women's side!
I did not dare to lift my eyes: I felt more fear than pride,
Till, "in the presence of the Lord," he said, and then there came
A holy strength upon my heart, and I could say the same.

XI.

I used to blush when he came near, but then I showed no sign;
With all the meeting looking on, I held his hand in mine.
It seemed my bashfulness was gone, now I was his for life:
Thee knows the feeling, Hannah, — thee, too, hast been a wife.

2

XII.

As home we rode, I saw no fields look half so green as ours ;
The woods were coming into leaf, the meadows full of flowers :
The neighbors met us in the lane, and every face was kind, —
'T is strange how lively everything comes back upon my mind.

XIII.

I see, as plain as thee sits there, the wedding dinner spread :
At our own table we were guests, with father at the head,
And Dinah Passmore helped us both, — 't was she stood up with me,
And Abner Jones with Benjamin, — and now they 're gone, all three !

XIV.

It is not right to wish for death ; the Lord disposes best.
His Spirit comes to quiet hearts, and fits them for his rest :
And that He halved our little flock was merciful, I see :
For Benjamin has two in heaven, and two are left with me.

XV.

Eusebius never cared to farm, — 't was not his call, in truth,
And I must rent the dear old place, and go to daughter Ruth.
Thee 'll say her ways are not like mine, — young people nowadays
Have fallen sadly off, I think, from all the good old ways.

XVI.

But Ruth is still a Friend at heart; she keeps the simple tongue,
The cheerful, kindly nature we loved when she was young;
And it was brought upon my mind, remembering her, of late,
That we on dress and outward things perhaps lay too much weight.

XVII.

I once heard Jesse Kersey say, a spirit clothed with grace,
And pure, almost, as angels are, may have a homely face.
And dress may be of less account; the Lord will look within:
The soul it is that testifies of righteousness or sin.

XVIII.

Thee must n't be too hard on Ruth: she's anxious I should go,
And she will do her duty as a daughter should, I know.
'T is hard to change so late in life, but we must be resigned:
The Lord looks down contentedly upon a willing mind.

THE HOLLY TREE

THE HOLLY-TREE.

I.

THE corn was warm in the ground, the fences were mended and made,
And the garden-beds, as smooth as a counterpane is laid,
Were dotted and striped with green where the peas and radishes grew,
With elecampane at the foot, and comfrey, and sage, and rue.

II.

The work was done on the farm, 't was orderly everywhere,
And comfort smiled from the earth, and rest was felt in the air.
When a Saturday afternoon at such a time comes round,
The farmer's fancies grow, as grows the grain in his ground.

III.

'T was so with Gabriel Parke : he stood by the holly-tree
That came, in the time of Penn, with his fathers over the sea :
A hundred and eighty years it had grown where it first was set,
And the thorny leaves were thick and the trunk was sturdy yet.

IV.

From the knoll where stood the house the fair fields pleasantly rolled
To dells where the laurels hung, and meadows of butter-cup gold :
He looked on them all by turns, with joy in his acres free,
But ever his thoughts came back to the tale of the holly-tree.

V.

In beautiful Warwickshire, beside the Avon stream,
John Parke, in his English home, had dreamed a singular dream.
He went with a sorrowful heart, for love of a bashful maid,
And a vision came as he slept one day in a holly's shade.

VI.

An angel sat in the boughs, and showed him a goodly land,
With hills that fell to a brook, and forests on either hand,
And said : " Thou shalt wed thy love, and this shall belong to you ;
For the earth has ever a home for a tender heart and true ! "

VII.

Even so it came to pass, as the angel promised then :
He wedded and wandered forth with the earliest friends of Penn,
And the home foreshown he found, with all that a home endears, —
A nest of plenty and peace, for a hundred and eighty years !

VIII.

In beautiful Warwickshire the life of the two began, —
A slip of the tree of the dream, a far-off sire of the man ;
And it seemed to Gabriel Parke, as the leaves above him stirred,
That the secret dream of his heart the soul of the holly heard.

IX.

Of Patience Phillips he thought : she, too, was a bashful maid :
The blue of her eyes was hid by the eyelash's golden shade ;
But well that she could not hide the checks that were fair to see
As the pink of an apple-bud, ere the blossom snows the tree!

X.

Ah! how had the English Parke to the English girl betrayed,
Save a dream had helped his heart, the love that makes afraid ? —
That seemed to smother his voice, when his blood so sweetly ran,
And the baby heart lay weak in the rugged breast of the man ?

XI.

His glance came back from the hills and back from the laurel glen,
And fell on the grass at his feet, where clucked a mother hen,
With a brood of tottering chicks, that followed as best they might ;
But one was trodden and lame, and drooped in a woful plight.

XII.

He lifted up from the grass the feeble, chittering thing,
And warmed its breast at his lips, and smoothed its stumpy wing,
When, lo! at his side a voice: " Is it hurt?" was all she said;
But the eyes of both were shy, and the cheeks of both were red.

XIII.

She took from his hand the chick, and fondled and soothed it then,
While, knowing that good was meant, cheerfully clucked the hen;
And the tongues of the two were loosed: there seemed a wonderful charm
In talk of the hatching fowls and spring-work done on the farm.

XIV.

But Gabriel saw that her eyes were drawn to the holly-tree:
" Have you heard," he said, ' how it came with the family over the sea?"
He told the story again, though he knew she knew it well,
And a spark of hope, as he spake, like fire in his bosom fell.

XV.

" I dreamed a beautiful dream, here, under the tree, just now,"
He said; and Patience felt the warmth of his eyes on her brow:
" I dreamed, like the English Parke; already the farm I own,
But the rest of the dream is best — the land is little, alone."

XVI.

He paused, and looked at the maid : her flushing cheek was bent,
And, under her chin, the chick was cheeping its warm content ;
But naught she answered — then he : " O Patience ! I thought of you !
Tell me you take the dream, and help me to make it true ! "

XVII.

The mother looked from the house, concealed by the window-pane,
And she felt that the holly's spell had fallen upon the twain ;
She guessed from Gabriel's face what the words he had spoken were,
And blushed in the maiden's stead, as if they were spoken to her

XVIII.

She blushed, and she turned away, ere the trembling man and maid
Silently hand in hand had kissed in the holly's shade,
And Patience whispered at last, her sweet eyes dim with dew :
" O Gabriel ! *could* you dream as much as I 've dreamed of you ? "

XIX.

The mother said to herself, as she sat in her straight old chair :
" He 's got the pick of the flock, so tidy and kind and fair !
At first I shall find it hard, to sit and be still, and see
How the house is kept to rights by somebody else than me.

XX.

"But the home must be theirs alone : I 'll do by her, if I can,
  As Gabriel's grandmother did, when I as a wife began :
  So good and faithful he 's been, from the hour when I gave him life,
  He shall master be in the house, and mistress shall be his wife !"

JOHN REED.

There's a mist on the meadow below; the herring-frogs chirp and cry;
It's chill when the sun is down, and the sod is not yet dry:
The world is a lonely place, it seems, and I don't know why.

I see, as I lean on the fence, how wearily trudges Dan
With the feel of the spring in his bones, like a weak and elderly man;
I've had it a many a time, but we must work when we can.

But' day after day to toil, and ever from sun to sun,
Though up to the season's front and nothing be left undone,
Is ending at twelve like a clock, and beginning again at one.

The frogs make a sorrowful noise, and yet it's the time they mate;
There's something comes with the spring, a lightness or else a weight;
There's something comes with the spring, and it seems to me it's fate.

It 's the hankering after a life that you never have learned to know ;
It 's the discontent with a life that is always thus and so ;
It 's the wondering what we are, and where we are going to go.

My life is lucky enough, I fancy, to most men's eyes,
For the more a family grows, the oftener some one dies,
And it 's now run on so long, it could n't be otherwise.

And Sister Jane and myself, we have learned to claim and yield ;
She rules in the house at will, and I in the barn and field,
So, nigh upon thirty years ! — as if written and signed and sealed.

I could n't change if I would ; I 've lost the how and the when ;
One day my time will be up, and Jane be the mistress then,
For single women are tough, and live down the single men.

She kept me so to herself, she was always the stronger hand,
And my lot showed well enough, when I looked around in the land ;
But I 'm tired and sore at heart, and I don't quite understand.

I wonder how it had been if I 'd taken what others need,
The plague, they say, of a wife, the care of a younger breed ?
If Edith Pleasanton now were with me as Edith Reed ?

Suppose that a son well grown were there in the place of Dan,
And I felt myself in him, as I was when my work began?
I should feel no older, sure, and certainly more a man!

A daughter, besides, in the house; nay, let there be two or three!
We never can overdo the luck that can never be,
And what has come to the most might also have come to me.

I 've thought, when a neighbor's wife or his child was carried away,
That to have no loss was a gain; but now, — I can hardly say;
He seems to possess them still, under the ridges of clay.

And share and share in a life is, somehow, a different thing
From property held by deed, and the riches that oft take wing;
I feel so close in the breast! — I think it must be the spring.

I 'm drying up like a brook when the woods have been cleared around;
You 're sure it must always run, you are used to the sight and sound,
But it shrinks till there 's only left a stony rut in the ground.

There 's nothing to do but take the days as they come and go,
And not to worry with thoughts that nobody likes to show,
For people so seldom talk of the things they want to know.

There 's times when the way is plain, and everything nearly right,
And then, of a sudden, you stand like a man with a clouded sight :
A bush seems often a beast, in the dusk of the falling night.

I must move ; my joints are stiff ; the weather is breeding rain,
And Dan is hurrying on with his plough-team up the lane.
I 'll go to the village store ; I 'd rather not talk with Jane.

. JANE REED.

" If I could forget," she said, " forget, and begin again!
We see so dull at the time, and, looking back, so plain:
There's a quiet that's worse, I think, than many a spoken strife,
And it's wrong that one mistake should change the whole of a life.

" There's John, forever the same, so steady, sober, and mild ;
He never storms as a man who never cried as a child :
Perhaps my ways are harsh, but if he would seem to care,
There'd be fewer swallowed words and a lighter load to bear.

" Here, Cherry! — she's found me out, the calf I raised in the spring,
And a likely heifer she's grown, the foolish, soft-eyed thing!
Just the even color I like, without a dapple or speck, —
O Cherry, bend down your head, and let me cry on your neck!

"The poor dumb beast she is, she never can know nor tell,
  And it seems to do me good, the very shame of the spell :
  So old a woman and hard, and Joel so old a man. —
  But the thoughts of the old go on as the thoughts of the young began !

"It's guessing that wastes the heart, far worse than the surest fate :
  If I knew he had thought of me, I could quietly work and wait ;
  And then when either, at last, on a bed of death should lie,
  Why, one might speak the truth, and the other hear and die !"

She leaned on the heifer's neck ; the dry leaves fell from the boughs,
  And over the sweet late grass of the meadow strayed the cows :
  The golden dodder meshed the cardinal-flower by the rill ;
  There was autumn haze in the air, and sunlight low on the hill.

"I've somehow missed my time," she said to herself and sighed :
"What girls are free to hope, a steady woman must hide,
  But the need outstays the chance : it makes me cry and laugh,
  To think that the only thing I can talk to now is a calf !"

A step came down from the hill: she did not turn or rise ;
There was something in her heart that saw without the eyes.
She heard the foot delay, as doubting to stay or go :
" Is the heifer for sale ? " he said.   She sternly answered, " No ! "

.

She lifted her head as she spoke : their eyes a moment met,
And her heart repeated the words, " If I could only forget ! "
He turned a little away, but her lowered eyes could see
His hand, as it picked the bark from the trunk of a hickory-tree.

.

" Why can't we be friendly, Jane ? " his words came, strange and slow ;
" You seem to bear me a grudge, so long, and so long ago !
You were gay and free with the rest, but always so shy of me,
That, before my freedom came, I saw that it could n't be."

" Joel ! " was all she cried, as their glances met again,
And a sudden rose effaced her pallor of age and pain.
He picked at the hickory bark : " It 's a curious thing to say ;
But I 'm lonely since Phœbe died and the girls are married away.

"That's why these thoughts come back: I'm a little too old for pride,
And I never could understand how love should be all one side:
'T would answer itself, I thought, and time would show me how;
But it didn't come so, then, and it doesn't seem so, now!"

"Joel, it came so, then!"—and her voice was thick with tears:
"A hope for a single day, and a bitter shame for years!"
He snapped the ribbon of bark; he turned from the hickory-tree:
"Jane, look me once in the face, and say that you thought of me!"

She looked, and feebly laughed: "It's a comfort to know the truth,
Though the chance was thrown away in the blind mistake of youth."
"And a greater comfort, Jane," he said, with a tender smile,
"To find the chance you have lost, and keep it a little while."

She rose as he spake the words: the petted heifer thrust
Her muzzle between the twain, with an animal's strange mistrust:
But over the creature's neck he drew her to his breast:
"A horse is never so old but it pulls with another best!"

THE OLD PENNSYLVANIA FARMER.

I.

WELL — well! this is a comfort, now — the air is mild as May,
And yet 't is March the twentieth, or twenty-first, to-day :
And Reuben ploughs the hill for corn ; I thought it would be tough,
But now I see the furrows turned, I guess it 's dry enough.

II.

I don't half live, penned up in doors ; a stove 's not like the sun.
When I can't see how things go on, I fear they 're badly done :
I might have farmed till now, I think — one's family is so queer —
As if a man can't oversee who 's in his eightieth year !

III.

Father, I mind, was eighty-five before he gave up his ;
But he was dim o' sight and crippled with the rheumatiz.
I followed in the old, steady way, so he was satisfied ;
But Reuben likes new-fangled things and ways I can't abide.

IV.

I 'm glad I built this southern porch ; my chair seems easier here :
I have n't seen as fine a spring this five-and-twenty year !
And how the time goes round so quick ! — a week, I would have sworn,
Since they were husking on the flat, and now they plough for corn !

V.

When I was young, time had for me a lazy ox's pace,
But now it 's like a blooded horse, that means to win the race.
And yet I can't fill out my days, I tire myself with naught ;
I 'd rather use my legs and hands than plague my head with thought.

VI.

There 's Marshall, too, I see from here : he and his boys begin.
Why don't they take the lower field ? that one is poor and thin.
A coat of lime it ought to have, but they 're a doless set :
They think swamp-mud 's as good, but we shall see what corn they get !

VII.

Across the level, Brown's new place begins to make a show ;
I thought he 'd have to wait for trees, but, bless me, how they grow !
They say it 's fine — two acres filled with evergreens and things ;
But so much land ! it worries me, for not a cent it brings.

VIII.

He has the right, I don't deny, to please himself that way,
But 't is a bad example set, and leads young folks astray :
Book-learning gets the upper-hand and work is slow and slack,
And they that come long after us will find things gone to wrack.

IX.

Now Reuben 's on the hither side; his team comes back again ;
I know how deep he sets the share, I see the horses strain :
I had that field so clean of stones, but he must plough so deep,
He 'll have it like a turnpike soon, and scarcely fit for sheep.

X.

If father lived, I 'd like to know what he would say to these
New notions of the younger men, who farm by chemistries :
There 's different stock and other grass ; there 's patent plough and cart —
Five hundred dollars for a bull ! it would have broke his heart.

XI.

The maples must be putting out : · I see a something red
Down yonder where the clearing laps across the meadow's head.
Swamp-cabbage grows beside the run ; the green is good to see,
But wheat's the color, after all, that cheers and 'livens me.

XII.

They think I have an easy time, no need to worry now —
Sit in the porch all day and watch them mow, and sow, and plough:
Sleep in the summer in the shade, in winter in the sun —
I'd rather do the thing myself, and know just how it's done!

XIII.

Well — I suppose I'm old, and yet 'tis not so long ago
When Reuben spread the swath to dry, and Jesse learned to mow,
And William raked, and Israel hoed, and Joseph pitched with me :
But such a man as I was then my boys will never be!

XIV.

I don't mind William's hankering for lectures and for books;
He never had a farming knack — you'd seé it in his looks ;
But handsome is that handsome does, and he is well to do:
'T would ease my mind if I could say the same of Jesse, too.

XV.

There's one black sheep in every flock, so there must be in mine,
But I was wrong that second time his bond to undersign :
It's less than what his share will be — but there's the interest!
In ten years more I might have had two thousand to invest.

XVI.

There's no use thinking of it now, and yet it makes me sore ;
The way I've slaved and saved, I ought to count a little more.
I never lost a foot of land, and that's a comfort, sure,
And if they do not call me rich, they cannot call me poor.

XVII.

Well, well ! ten thousand times I've thought the things I'm thinking now ;
I've thought them in the harvest-field and in the clover mow ;
And often I get tired of them, and wish I'd something new —
But this is all I've had and known ; so what's a man to do ?

XVIII.

'Tis like my time is nearly out, of that I'm not afraid ;
I never cheated any man, and all my debts are paid.
They call it rest that we shall have, but work would do no harm ;
There can't be rivers there and fields, without some sort o' farm !